Hachette UK's policy is to use papers that are natural, renewable and recyclable products and made from wood grown in well-managed forests and other controlled sources. The logging and manufacturing processes are expected to conform to the environmental regulations of the country of origin.

ISBN: 9781398325616

First published in 2022 by Hodder & Stoughton Limited (for its Rising Stars imprint, part of the Hodder Education Group)
An Hachette UK Company
Carmelite House, 50 Victoria Embankment, London EC4Y 0DZ
www.risingstars-uk.com

Impression number 10 9 8 7 6 5 4 3 2 1
Year 2026 2025 2024 2023 2022

Author: Gill Lewis
Series Editor: Tony Bradman
Commissioning Editor: Hamish Baxter
Illustrator: Ana Sebastián/Bright Group International
Educational Reviewer: Helen Marron
Design concept and layout: Lynda Murray
Editor: Amy Tyrer

With thanks to the schools that took part in the development of *Reading Planet* KS2, including: Ancaster CE Primary School, Ancaster; Downsway Primary School, Reading; Ferry Lane Primary School, London; Foxborough Primary School, Slough; Griffin Park Primary School, Blackburn; St Barnabas CE First & Middle School, Pershore; Tranmoor Primary School, Doncaster; and Wilton CE Primary School, Wilton.

A catalogue record for this title is available from the British Library.

Printed in the UK.

Orders: Please contact Hachette UK Distribution, Hely Hutchinson Centre, Milton Road, Didcot, Oxfordshire, OX11 7HH.
Telephone: (44) 01235 400555. Email: primary@hachette.co.uk.

MIX
Paper from responsible sources
FSC™ C104740

Contents

Some people say crows are evil.

Some say they bring death and disease.

Some say they are omens of bad luck.

But I say they haven't met Kevin.

He's my crow.

Well, he's not exactly my crow. He's a wild crow. You can't really own a wild crow.

I suppose he's my friend.

I saved him after he fell out of his nest as a chick and was bitten by a dog. I took him home to feed him until he learned to fly. And then I let him go. But he always recognises me. Sometimes, he even follows me to school. He lives in the big oak tree in the middle of the Crow Field.

It's how the Crow Field got its name – because crows like to nest in the oak and the other tall trees at the top of the field. It's where people walk their dogs and where we kick a ball about at weekends. Some people jog around the paths, and others picnic on the wide, grassy areas. When I was younger, my sister and I used to catch grasshoppers in the long grasses at the edges of the field before letting them go.

So, I'm here, walking on my way to school and I hear Kevin. I look up and find him flying above me.

"Caw ... caw ... caaaaw!"

Then he flaps down and follows me, swooping along the walls and resting on telegraph poles. He looks me right in the eye too, turning his head on his side. People think crows are ugly, but they haven't looked at crows properly. His feathers aren't just black. They shine with the deepest blue, like a midnight sky.

They're the most intelligent birds too. I read that they can recognise human faces and know how you're feeling. Kevin always seems to know when I am sad or lonely. Mind you, that's happened quite a lot since Carter and his mates decided it was my turn to be bullied by them. Kevin doesn't like them. He swoops down at them when they pick on me. And now Carter and his mates call me 'Birdbrain', instead of my real name, Ash. Maybe it's easier to bully someone if you don't use their name.

Sometimes, I wish Kevin was six feet tall. I saw a wildlife documentary where a massive stork swallowed a frog whole. I wish Kevin could swallow Carter whole. I can imagine it. I can see Kevin gulping Carter down, his brand-new trainers and all.

But Kevin is only a crow. He's not big enough to eat Carter. And Carter is far too clever to be caught.

And here they are again.

Carter, Aiden and Josh.

Waiting for me at the bus stop.

The bus has been and gone, and so it's just them, me and Kevin.

And I've got nowhere to escape to.

Carter leans against the wall, a mean smile across his face. “All right, Ash?” he says, and then looks up at Kevin, who is perched on a nearby telegraph pole. “I see you’ve brought your friend along too.”

I keep my head down, but Aiden steps in front of me, blocking my path.

“Hey, Birdbrain!” Aiden puts his hand out. “What have you got for us today?”

My mouth goes dry. “Nothing,” I say.

“Come on,” says Aiden, pushing his hand nearer. “Rules are rules. And *we* make the rules.”

I put my hand in my back pocket and pull out a few coins. I put them in Aiden’s hand.

"Come on, Ash," Carter says. "Doesn't your mum let you have more pocket money than that?"

I feel sick inside. I took the money from Mum's purse without her knowing. I don't get any pocket money. Mum can't afford it. And it's not like Carter needs the money. His dad's rich. He buys him the latest trainers, phones and computer games. But this isn't about the money. Carter likes pushing people around. He wants to be in control.

Josh shoves me in the back. "What else you got?"

"That's it," I say.

Josh pulls my bag off my back and looks inside. "Nothing at all?"

I shake my head.

He empties the contents on the wet ground and opens my pencil case.

"Ooh! What have we got here?" he says, holding up the chocolate bar I'd hidden. "Did you forget this?"

I say nothing.

Josh throws it to Carter.

"My favourite chocolate," Carter says, catching it. "How did you know?"

I stare at the ground.

Carter eats most of it and throws the rest for Aiden and Josh to share.

"*Caw ... caw ... caw!*" caws Kevin.

Carter looks up. "Can't you shut your bird up?"

Josh picks up a stone and flings it at Kevin.

"NO!" I yell. And I'm glad Kevin flaps away in the direction of the Crow Field.

"We're done here," says Carter. He walks away and drops the chocolate wrapper on the ground. "Hey, Birdbrain. Pick it up. Littering is bad for the environment."

Aiden laughs out loud.

And then they are gone, walking ahead of me.

People think bullies come in one size – with big fists and small brains.

But bullies come in all sizes.

Carter keeps his hands clean and gets his mates to do the nasty work. He's clever. Not brainy clever, but he's smart. He's good with words. He can talk his way in or out of everything.

He makes people laugh. And I don't know why they seem to like him, because his jokes are usually mean.

I see them standing near the school gates. I don't want to walk past them. I don't want to be anywhere near them. Then I hear the school bell, and I know I'll be marked as late.

I don't want to go to school.

I can't go home or Mum will be mad at me.

There's only one place I want to be.

Up the old oak with Kevin.

Up in my Crow Tree.

I keep in the shadows and jog around the back of the school and out on to the road that goes past the supermarket.

Soon, I reach the hedge next to the Crow Field. I look to make sure I can't see anyone and then I walk across the path through the field. The path passes right beneath the big oak tree. My Crow Tree. Its trunk is so thick that it takes three people with their arms stretched wide to circle it.

It's early April and tiny new leaves are unfurling on the tree. I look up into the branches. They are high and out of reach. Nobody ever climbs this tree.

Nobody.

Except me. I know exactly which cracks in the bark to hook my fingers into and which knots to put my feet against. I check no one is watching, and then I take a running jump and swing myself up into the branches.

I climb higher and higher until I find my sitting place in a fork of the trunk. The tree was hit by lightning many years ago and part of the trunk is now hollow. If I tuck myself in here, I can hide from people on the ground and shelter from the rain.

I keep a store of food in a tin here, and I have an old coat to keep me warm.

It's my secret place, and it's the best place in the world.

"Caw! Caw! Caw!"

I look up and smile.

Kevin is perched in the high branches at the top of the tree. Another crow arrives – it's Kevin's mate. They nested in this tree last year and raised three chicks last summer.

I reach into my snack tin
and pull out a biscuit. I hold some of it
out on my hand and wait. Kevin comes
down next to me and sits on a branch.
He tips his head on its side and looks at me.
I push my hand nearer to him, and he
reaches out and takes the biscuit crumbs.

"Caw!" says Kevin.

I'm sure he knows how I'm feeling. I smile.
"I'm okay, Kevin. Carter's a jerk, though,
isn't he?"

"Caaaaw!" says Kevin as if he's agreeing.

Kevin isn't the only animal in this tree. There are often squirrels. There were two baby squirrels last year that raced and chased each other in circles up and down the branches.

A magpie sometimes comes to squawk at the crows.

There's a tiny brown bird, as small as a mouse, that spirals up and down. It digs its small beak into the bark looking for insects. I looked up its name on my phone, and it's called a treecreeper.

A black and white woodpecker sometimes drums at the deadwood of the broken trunk. And in summer there are so many insects that the whole tree hums with them.

When I'm up here, I sit so still that none of the animals notice me. It's weird really. I almost feel I'm part of the tree.

Loads of people pass by, but they don't know I'm up here. I watch them all from here. There's an old lady in a long, green coat who walks her scruffy little dog. On weekdays, a group of nursery children come to play, and at weekends I sometimes see kids from school playing football on the pitch.

But no one knows I'm here.

No one can find me.

For now, I'm safe and I can forget all about school and Carter and his mates.

Somewhere, far away, an ice-cream van tinkles its tune. A squirrel scuttles up the tree and the breeze sighs through the branches.

I wrap the old coat around me, curl up in the hollow trunk and close my eyes.

The spring sunshine warms me, and before I know it, I'm drifting off to sleep.

I wake to my phone buzzing in my pocket.

It's a text from Mum.

> Ash! Where are you? School says you didn't turn up today.

It buzzes again.

> ASH! If you don't answer, I'll call the police. I'm worried.

I grunt and answer.

> I'm okay. I'll come back home.

The old lady in the green coat is walking beneath the tree. I wait for her to pass by, and then I drop down to the ground.

I walk home, head down.

Kevin follows me, stopping at the hedge at the border of the field. He lands and caws at me.

I turn around. “I’ll be back tomorrow,” I say.

I slow down as I get closer to home.

I know Mum will be mad at me.

“Where were you?” says Mum. She’s in the kitchen.

I just stare at the floor. “I was just out.”

“Why did you miss school?” Mum asks.

I shrug.

Mum pours a cup of tea and sits down. “Is something wrong, Ash?”

I shake my head. I don’t want to talk about it.

Mum takes a sip of tea, not taking her eyes from me. “Your teacher said you’ve not been handing in homework.”

“It’s boring,” I say.

“He said you’re just not focused,” says Mum.

“Well, he’s a jerk,” I snap. Mum slams her tea down, making it slop across the table. “Ash! What’s got into you?”

I can’t tell her I’m avoiding Carter and his mates. I’ll only be picked on more if Mum gets involved.

I push past her and go up the stairs. “Leave me alone.”

“Ash!” calls Mum.

But I close the door to my bedroom and sit on the bed. I rummage in my bedside drawers hoping to find some coins to pay Carter tomorrow, but I can’t find any. I don’t want to go back downstairs, so I climb into bed and pull my duvet over me, but sleep won’t come. I just lie awake, dreading school again tomorrow.

I wake and groan.

Another school day.

One more day until the weekend, and then I'll have two whole days away from Carter. I hear my sister, Mimi, in the bathroom, and I slip into her room and empty her piggybank of coins. It's not much, but I hope she won't notice. She only plays with it like pretend money anyway.

In the kitchen, Mum watches me grab a piece of toast and head out of the door. "The school said they'd ring me so I know you've been to registration," she says.

I nod and step out into the bright sunshine. I don't go via the Crow Field because I don't want Kevin following me to school. I don't want Carter and his mates to hurt him. So, I go a different way, past the church.

As I get near school, I see Carter, Aiden and Josh surrounding Mia from our class. They've emptied her bag and are looking for food and money. Mia's trying to fight back, but it's three against one and they are bigger than her.

I see her homework drop on to the wet ground. When Josh can't find what he's looking for, he puts his foot on her homework and mashes it into a puddle.

Mia picks up her reading book from the ground and hurls it at Aiden. He flinches, then picks it up and tosses it over the wall into the churchyard. I hear Carter laugh.

Mia looks across at me, and I hurry on. But I know she saw me, watching.

In class, Mr Williams asks for our homework. I give mine to him, but when he reaches Mia she just stares at the table.

"I don't have it," she says.

Mr Williams frowns. "Why not?"

"I lost it," she says.

I hear Aiden snigger.

"Well, you'll have to do it again," says Mr Williams. "Make sure you bring it in tomorrow," he says. "Now, everyone, get out your reading books."

I see Mia sink her head lower.

"Where's your book, Mia?" says Mr Williams.

"I don't have it, either," says Mia.

"I hope you haven't lost that too," says Mr Williams.

I hear Carter get up from his seat and watch him put his own book on Mia's desk.

"She can borrow mine," says Carter. "Aiden and I will share."

“Thank you, Carter,” says Mr Williams. “That’s kind of you. At least someone’s got their head screwed on today.”

Mia’s face is red with anger.

It’s not fair.

But I don’t say anything, and it makes me feel weak inside.

This is how Carter and his mates get away with it all the time.

When the bell goes for lunchtime, I head out of class and go to the library. It's safe in the library. Carter doesn't go there. I see Mia hunched in the corner. I guess that's why she's here too. I feel bad for not sticking up for her in class.

"You okay?" I say.

She scowls at me. "What do you want?"

I sit down opposite her. "I'll go to Mr Williams and tell him I saw Carter trash your homework."

"Don't," says Mia. "It'll make it worse."

"Maybe we've got to fight this together," I say.

Mia rolls her eyes. "What, just me and you? No one else is going to say anything. They're too scared of Carter. Just leave it."

At home time, I slip out of the back of school and run. Mia's right. What could I do? Carter would just make it worse for both of us if I had stood up for Mia. I hate him. I hate school. I just want to be safe in my Crow Tree where Carter can't catch me.

But when I get to the Crow Field, I can't get in.

There are loads of vans and a big crane in the middle of the field next to my Crow Tree.

Men in high-vis jackets are pulling massive green nets across all the hedges and a net right over the Crow Tree.

I try to step into the field, but one man blocks my path.

“Sorry, sonny, you can’t go in today,” he says.

“What’s going on?” I ask.

“These hedges and the tree need to be taken down,” he says.

I look at the ugly thick plastic netting. “Why?”

“Because they do,” he says.

“But why?” I say again. He’s getting impatient.

“The council is redeveloping the Crow Field. It’s going to be made into an out-of-town retail centre,” says the man. “We need to remove the tree and hedges soon. We have to put netting across to stop the birds nesting, otherwise we can’t remove the tree.”

“You can’t take the oak tree down,” I say.

The man looks annoyed. “What’s it to you?”

“You just can’t.” I think of Kevin and his mate already starting to build their nest.

"I won't let you," I say, but it sounds so feeble when I say it.

Even the man laughs. "Well, sonny," he says, "it's not up to me. It's up to the council. They make the rules. And rules are rules. Now, move along. I've got work to do."

He gets into his van, and I stand back as he drives into the field. I watch the crane lift the net up high and over the big oak. My oak.

I see Kevin and his mate wheeling around in the sky, cawing.

I feel so helpless. There is nothing I can do.

I walk away from him, looking back over my shoulder. I have to walk all the way around the Crow Field now, alongside the busy road thick with traffic fumes and noise.

I see the old lady in the long, green coat walking her small dog along the pavement. She's looking at the netted hedges too. She stops, as if she's about to say something to me, but I keep my head down and hurry on.

I walk all the way around to the other side. Kevin doesn't seem to see me. He and his mate keep circling high, cawing loudly. They can't get into their tree with the big net over it.

I don't know where he'll go. The tree is his home. It's home for all the other creatures too.

If the tree is cut down, I'll lose my special place.

If it's cut down, I'll lose Kevin.

And I hear those horrible words again. They are the words that Aiden said: *Rules are rules. And we make the rules.*

And I feel even more helpless than before.

I don't even feel like getting out of bed.

It's Saturday. Usually, I'd go to the Crow Field, but I don't want to see those green nets again. But Mimi is grumpy with a cold, and I know Mum will get me to tidy my room, so I pull on my jumper and head out of the door.

When I get there, the workmen and the vehicles have gone, but the nets cover all the hedges and the tree. There are people walking their dogs, and I see some kids from my year kicking a football around.

I don't feel like joining them. I want to see if Kevin is okay. There's so much netting. I don't want to imagine this place as a retail centre with shops and car parks. I hate to think of the hedges ripped out and concrete across the grass. Where will we walk? Where will we play? Where will the wild animals live? No one seems to have noticed, except me. It's like they are blindfolded. Maybe they don't care. Maybe they just think there is nothing they can do.

I walk up to the Crow Tree, looking up into the branches. It's like the netting has trapped the whole tree. Maybe it's because I'm looking up that, at first, I don't see three people on the other side of the tree trunk.

It's Carter, Aiden and Josh.

I'm about to turn away when I hear an alarm call.

"CAW ... CAW ... CAW!"

Something is flapping in the net above their heads.

"CAW ... CAW ... CAW!"

It's Kevin. Somehow, he's got inside the net, and his feet are stuck. He's struggling to get free.

Josh jumps up and pulls the netting, but he can't quite reach him.

Aiden picks up a stone and throws it. The stone misses, and Kevin caws again, louder this time. He sounds scared.

Josh picks up another stone.

"No!" I yell.

They all turn to look at me.

"Leave him alone," I shout.

A nasty smile crosses Carter's face. "Well, if it isn't Birdbrain!"

"Leave him," I yell again.

Carter grins. He takes the stone from Josh and throws it up and down in his hand, as if he's weighing it. "And how are you going to stop us, Birdbrain?" Carter says.

I can see that Kevin's frightened. His feathers look battered and ruffled against the net.

Carter takes a step closer and raises his arm, ready to throw. I launch forward but feel myself pulled back by Aiden. I sprawl on the floor and see the stone fly from Carter's hand. The stone hits Kevin, and he squawks and flaps even harder. I don't know if he's hurt.

"Stop it," I yell as Aiden holds me down.

And I'm crying now. I'm angry at myself because my crying makes them laugh.

I try to struggle away from Aiden, but Josh helps pin me down too.

Carter reaches for the stone again. Kevin has fallen further down the netting. He's within easy reach now.

"Say goodbye to your friend," laughs Carter.

"No," I scream. "NO!"

Chapter 7

I close my eyes. I don't want to see Kevin being hurt. But I hear a yell. I open my eyes and Carter is sprawling beside me. I look up to see Mia standing over him, swinging her bag round and round her head. She's knocked Carter right off his feet.

"Didn't you hear what he said?" she yells. "Leave the bird alone!"

"Get lost," shouts Carter. "This isn't your business."

Mia keeps swinging her bag so he can't get up. "Leave it!"

Josh grabs at Mia's bag and tries to pull it from her. "You're gonna be so sorry you did this."

Mia's clinging on to her bag. I'm struggling to get away from Aiden, and Kevin is still cawing. Then we hear a TAP ... TAP ... TAP, and a little dog runs up to us all, barking.

The old lady in the green coat and her dog have arrived, her stick tapping on the ground. She looks around at us all. "What's going on here?"

Carter is quick to answer. "Thank you for coming. This girl and her friend attacked us. We weren't doing anything."

The lady looks around at us all, then at Kevin, and then at me. Then she turns to Carter, Aiden and Josh. Her stare burns right into them, and for the first time I see Carter falter.

"I think you three had better get going," says the lady. "Now."

I watch Carter and wonder for a second if he's going to stand up to her, but he gets up, brushes his trousers down and walks away, with Josh and Aiden behind him. I hear him mutter something rude under his breath.

I rush forward to reach Kevin, scrambling under the net to get to him. I hold him gently while unhooking his claws from the netting. I take him out and sit down on a nearby bench. Mia and the old lady sit down beside me.

I check Kevin all over. I stretch out his wings and feel relieved that I can't find any breaks at all. Mia reaches into her bag and pulls out a biscuit. She holds it towards Kevin, and he pecks it from her hand.

"Thank you," I say. I wipe my tears. I feel silly for crying. "You didn't have to help. I didn't help you the other day."

"Well," says Mia. "I did some thinking. And you're right. The only way to fight them is to do it together."

"Yeah, us two and a crow," I say. "I'm not sure we outnumber Carter and his mates."

"Well, I reckoned if you were brave enough to help a crow, I could be brave enough to help you," says Mia.

"It was a brave thing you both did," says the old lady. "It's good to see young people looking after wildlife."

"His name's Kevin," I say. "I know it sounds silly. But I rescued him as a chick."

"That's cool," says Mia. "Can I hold him?"

I hand him over, hoping Kevin won't mind. He doesn't know her, but he seems fine with it. I think he must know when people are being kind.

"I think we can let him go," I say. "His mate's calling him."

Mia puts Kevin on the ground. He looks up, turning his head from side to side. Then he flies up to join his mate, and they circle round and round.

I look up into the tree and sigh. “He’s got nowhere to nest now,” I say. “The oak is being cut down.”

“It’s not fair,” says Mia. She watches Kevin high up, near the top of the tree, trying to get through the netting to the nest he’s been building. She takes her phone out and videos it. “This whole place is being made into a retail centre. There’ll be nowhere left for us to play, either.”

“I’ll miss this tree,” says the old lady. “It’s a great friend of mine.”

“Mine too,” I say.

“How old is it?” asks Mia.

“Over 250 years,” says the old lady.

“How do you know?” asks Mia.

“Well,” says the lady, “a friend of mine and I measured it. You can tell by measuring around the trunk.”

I try to imagine this town 250 years ago. “What was it like back then?”

The old lady smiles. "Well, it was a bit before my time too, dear. It was before electricity, cars and even steam trains."

"We can't let it be chopped down," says Mia.

The old lady sighs. "I wish I could save this tree. It saved my life."

We both look at her and say, "How?"

She smiles and says, "Perhaps I should tell you. You know, I used to be able to climb up into this tree, just like you."

"You've been up there?" I ask.

"Yes," she says. "I've seen you go up there too, putting your hands and feet into the same places I used to." She sighs. "Though I am 90 this year and can't do it any more."

"How did the tree save you?" asks Mia.

"Well, I'll tell you," says the lady. "But first I need you to get something I left up there a long time ago.

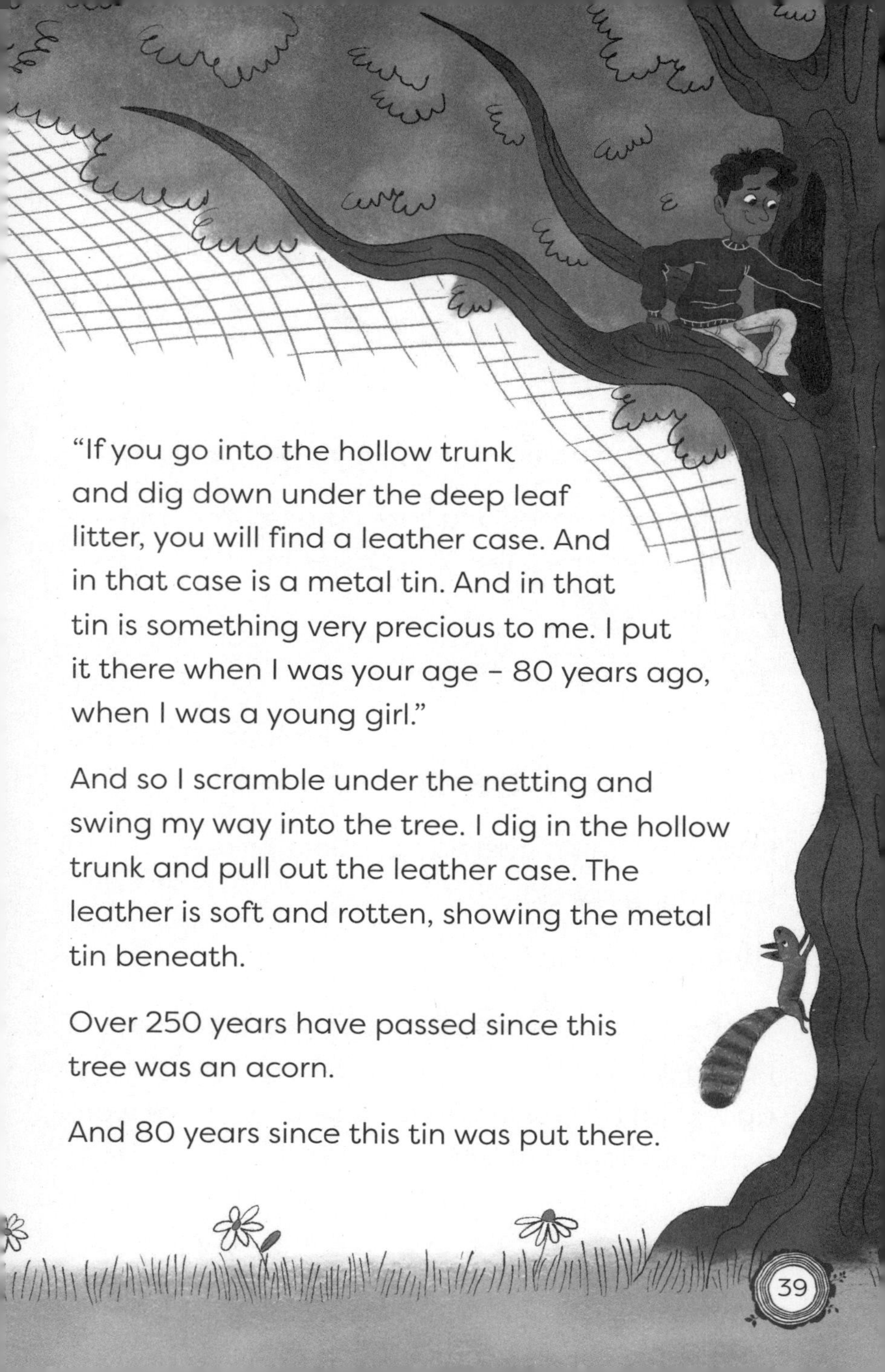

"If you go into the hollow trunk and dig down under the deep leaf litter, you will find a leather case. And in that case is a metal tin. And in that tin is something very precious to me. I put it there when I was your age – 80 years ago, when I was a young girl."

And so I scramble under the netting and swing my way into the tree. I dig in the hollow trunk and pull out the leather case. The leather is soft and rotten, showing the metal tin beneath.

Over 250 years have passed since this tree was an acorn.

And 80 years since this tin was put there.

I bring it down and sit with Mia and the old lady.

The old lady smiles and takes the tin from me. "I'm Gracie," she says. She strokes her dog's ears. "And this is Archie."

"I'm Ash," I say. "And this is Mia."

Gracie looks at the tin, and her hands are shaking. "It's a long, long time since I've seen this."

I stare at the tin, feeling I'm about to see something special.

"What's inside it?" asks Mia.

"I'd better tell you how it got up there before I open it," Gracie says. "It was a long, long time ago when this town was a lot smaller. There were fields all around here.

During the war, they thought this town was safe from German bombs, and so a boy was sent to live with a foster family near me. He was a Jew, named Otto, sent from Germany without his parents when Jews were trying to get their children away from the Nazis. Otto and I became good friends and always came up here. We both used to play in the tree too."

"That's so weird to think it's the same tree, but so long ago," I say.

Gracie smiles. "Time is a funny thing. It seems like only yesterday. Otto had a pet crow too. You reminded me of him when I saw you with your crow following you about."

"What happened to Otto?" asks Mia.

"Well, in that autumn near the end of the war, we found out that this town wasn't safe from the German planes. One afternoon, when Otto and I were playing in this field, German planes flew overhead. We had no warning. By the time the air raid sirens blared, we could see the planes. We had no time to get to our homes, so Otto and I climbed up into this tree, hoping it could protect us. Bombs started to drop. Lots of them. There was noise and smoke everywhere. The whole town seemed to be on fire. The tree kept us safe. But Otto's foster family was killed, and so Otto was sent far away to another family. I lost contact with him after that."

"You never spoke to him again?" asks Mia.

Gracie shakes her head. "I never found out where he went."

I stare at the box. "So, what's in there?"

Gracie opens the lid. She gently lifts out a long black feather. "This feather was from Otto's crow, the one that followed him around," she says.

I stare up at Kevin and his mate. I wonder if Otto's crow is an ancestor of Kevin.

Then Gracie takes a deep breath and pulls out a document. There's a photo of a young boy and lots of German words I don't understand.

But I see the name Otto Meyer next to the boy. She runs her finger across the boy's cheek. I see tears in Gracie's eyes. "Otto," she says. "This is my Otto. Otto Meyer."

"We should try to find him," I say.

Gracie sighs and shakes her head. "Otto was older than me. He might not even be alive."

We meet up again the next day at the park, Mia and I.

It's always busy near the football pitch on a Sunday, so Mia and I sit on the bench near the Crow Tree.

Mia shakes her head. "I can't find an Otto Meyer," she says. "I got Mum to help me search for him on the internet last night, but there's nothing about him."

"Look," I say, "here comes Gracie and Archie."

Gracie joins us and sits down with her dog.

"We couldn't find Otto," says Mia. "I'm sorry."

Gracie sighs. "Maybe it's for the best. He would be sad about this tree coming down."

I look up into the nets covering the Crow Tree. "But it's just wrong," I say.

"But it's the rules," says Mia glumly.

Gracie scratches Archie behind the ear. "Just because it's a rule, doesn't make it right," she says. "Sometimes, we have to stand up for what we believe is right."

"But what can we do?" I ask. "What can we do to stop the Crow Tree being chopped down?"

Gracie sighs. "Otto's family died because people stayed silent when the Nazis were rising to power. Sometimes, it takes one or two brave people to speak out first, before it's too late."

"We could stand outside the Crow Field with banners," says Mia.

"And we could make some leaflets," I say. "We can hand them out to people who use the Crow Field."

"But will it work?" says Mia.

Gracie smiles. “You won’t know until you try.”

“Right,” I say. “I’m going home to make the leaflets.”

Mia stands up. “And I’ll make banners.”

I look up into the tree. “Kevin,” I yell. “We’re going to save you. We’re going to save your tree.” Then I turn to Mia and Gracie. “Let’s meet at the entrance to the Crow Field at eight tomorrow morning, before we have to go to school.”

Then I’m off, running across the grass. And I almost feel like I’m flying, because it feels good to be actually doing something at last.

I work all evening on my leaflets.

I put a photo of Kevin on there and one of the Crow Tree. I write that we need the Crow Field for wildlife and people too, and I ask people to protest with us to stop the Crow Field being built upon.

When I go to print them out, we don't have that much ink in the printer, and I only manage to print about 30 leaflets before the ink runs out. I throw some of the ones that didn't come out well in the bin. Still, it's a start. I can always print some more.

The next morning, I grab the leaflets, put them in my bag and head out of the house early.

"Where are you going so early?" says Mum.

"Nowhere," I yell as I fly out of the door. I don't want to tell Mum what I'm doing. I bet she'd try to stop me if I did.

I'm out of breath when I meet Mia. She's made two big signs with the words:

She's even managed to find a hat with a crow on it to wear.

Everyone's in such a rush, they hardly notice us. They are on their way to work or school and pass us by, heads down, not wanting to stop. I try to hand out leaflets, but no one seems to want them.

No one seems to care at all.

And suddenly I feel really sad inside. If no one cares about a single crow, in a single tree, in a single field, how will they even care about the rest of the planet? It seems like no one cares about the world at all.

I feel the leaflets snatched from my hand.

It's Carter and his mates.

Carter looks us up and down. "What a pair of losers. Birdbrain and his girlfriend."

"Get lost," says Mia.

I try to grab my leaflets, but Carter throws them high in the air, where the wind whips them away and scatters them across the road.

Aiden tuts. "Littering again, Ash? It's not good for the environment, is it?"

I'm so angry that I don't notice the van at first. It's one of the vans with all the stuff to take the tree down. It beeps, and a man sticks his head out of the window.

"Hey, move it," says the man. "We're coming through."

Mia holds her banner up higher. "We won't let you."

I stand beside her and hold my banner up too. "We won't let you cut down the tree."

The man rolls his eyes and reverses, then drives away down the road.

I grin at Mia. "See, we can stop them."

Josh is sniggering, then he whispers something to Carter and Aiden.

"What's so funny?" I say.

Then Carter laughs out loud. He points at something behind me. "You forgot the other gate."

I spin around. The van has driven into the field through a different gate. It's parked near to the Crow Tree. Already, I can see two men in high-vis jackets getting chainsaws and tree-climbing gear out of the van.

Carter, Josh and Aiden are all laughing now.

Carter steps forward and gives me a shove. "By the time we get back from school, your Crow Tree won't be here at all."

I cover my ears, but I can't get their laughing out of my head. "Shut up," I yell. "SHUT UP!"

But it just makes them laugh even louder.

Josh flaps his hands like a crow. "Caw, caw, caw!" he calls.

I hear the sound of a chainsaw rev up beside the Crow Tree.

And I feel anger rise up inside me. Our banners and our leaflets haven't done anything at all. How can we save the Crow Tree now?

I do the only thing I can think of.

I run.

I run and run, my feet flying over the grass.

I run and run towards the Crow Tree.

I hear one of the men shout, but they don't have time to stop me. I slide underneath the netting. I leap and put my feet and hands into the knots and grooves I know so well, then I swing up into the tree. My Crow Tree.

I glare down at the men from the branches. "You can't cut the tree down now," I yell. "And you can't make me come down. You can't touch me. I'm staying here until I know the tree is safe."

A man in high-vis glares up at me. "Get down now, sonny," he shouts. "Or I'll call the police."

"I don't care," I shout back.

"You'll get hungry and want to come down soon enough," says the man.

But then I see Mia and Gracie coming towards me.

"You can have my packed lunch," shouts Mia. She tries to throw her lunchbox up to me, but the man raises his arms to stop her.

Gracie takes the lunchbox from her. "Ash!" Gracie calls.

And before I know it, Gracie is swinging her arm round in the air and the lunchbox is flying in a perfect curve towards me. I catch it just in time.

Gracie is grinning. "I used to play cricket on the women's team. Good to see I can still bowl a fast one!"

The man is getting angry now. "Look, we've got a job to do. Come down and stop mucking around. I'm calling the police."

Mia pulls out her phone. "And I'm calling the newspapers."

By lunchtime, there's quite a crowd around the tree. I've turned my phone off because I don't want Mum to know I'm here.

Mia's mum and dad are here – she phoned them to say she wasn't going to school. She said she's protesting, and they said they'd join her too. Gracie went home, but she's come back with a tin of biscuits and a flask of tea.

The police have arrived too, but they can't force me out of the tree.

And now it seems we've caught people's attention, because lots of people are coming into the Crow Field to find out what the fuss is about.

"Look," calls Mia. "Here comes a TV crew."

The TV crew set up their camera beneath the tree. The reporter from the evening news is here, wanting to find out why we are protesting. I see them interviewing Mia and then Gracie. I hear Gracie tell them all about how the tree saved her and her friend Otto Meyer. Then she shows them the photo of Otto when he was a boy.

Then the interviewer cranes his neck to look up at me. "Why are you saving the Crow Field, Ash?"

My mind goes blank. There are so many things I want to say, but all I can think is what I really feel. "I'm saving it for the crows. And for my crow friend, Kevin."

It's such a stupid thing to say. I bet people will laugh.

But just then, someone from the crowd shouts. "WE WANT KEVIN."

Then someone else shouts it too.

And soon everyone is chanting it. "WE WANT KEVIN! WE WANT KEVIN! WE WANT KEVIN!"

Then, just when I think things are going our way, Mum turns up.

She looks so angry.

She glares up into the tree. "I've only just found out you are up there," she shouts. "My phone's been off all day."

A policeman turns to her. "Is this your son?"

Mum nods.

“Well, can you get him down?” he asks.

Mum tuts loudly. “I’ll have to go and talk to him. Has anyone got a ladder?”

The high-vis man is only too happy to help. “Get him down from there, for goodness’ sake.”

The high-vis man puts the ladder against the trunk and holds it still for Mum to climb.

I watch her coming closer and closer.

She looks a bit different because she doesn’t usually wear jeans. And then I notice the heavy bag slung across her back. She heaves herself on to the branch beside me.

“I’m sorry, Mum ...” I begin.

Mum reaches into her bag and pulls out one of the crumpled leaflets I left in the bin.

“It’s a kind thing to look after something that can’t speak up for itself,” she says.

"So, you're not angry with me?" I ask.

"I'm not angry with you," says Mum. "I'm angry the council are destroying the Crow Field. In fact, I'm proud of you." She pulls some sandwiches and crisps from her bag. "So, I've come to join you too."

"Oi!" shouts the high-vis man. "When you've had your cosy chat, can you come on down?"

Mum leans over and looks down. "Not until the Crow Field is safe," she shouts back. "Now you've got two of us up here."

I'm not sure how long we can stay up here. There aren't exactly toilets in the tree. But Mum has even packed blankets in case we need to stay up here all night.

Mia goes home for tea, but then she comes back to tell us our protest has been put on the early evening news. She got her mum to start a petition to save the Crow Field, and in the first half hour it had 200 signatures.

Kevin is a bit of a celebrity now. People have turned up carrying placards with pictures of Kevin and '**SAVE KEVIN**' in big letters.

There's a chill in the air and I wrap a blanket around me. I don't know how you sleep in a tree without falling out. I'm hungry again too. This protesting isn't easy.

Mia's mum and dad buy us fish and chips, and Mum and I eat them in packets up in the tree.

We're happily munching our chips when a young woman arrives at the base of the tree. She takes out a pair of binoculars and points them right up into the branches.

"Do you mind?" says Mum. "We'd like a bit of privacy here."

The woman takes the binoculars from her eyes. "Sorry, I'm not looking at you. I'm looking up at the crows' nest."

I turn and look too. "That's Kevin and his mate's nest," I say.

She looks again through her binoculars. "I can't see if it's an active nest. Have they been using it this year?"

"I've seen them building it," I say. "My friend Mia took a video of it."

"Really?" says the woman. "Can I see it?"

Mia takes out her phone and shows her the video of Kevin building the nest.

A big grin breaks out across her face. "Could you share that with me?" she says. "If you do, we might just be able to save Kevin."

It's funny how some things happen so fast when you least expect them.

It turns out the woman with the binoculars is from a wildlife group. She saw the news and thought she saw the crows' nest in the tree. She says putting netting over a nest while birds are building it is against the law. No one is allowed to disturb a wild bird's nest.

She makes some phone calls. Then we see the two police officers coming across the field.

The man with the high-vis jacket nods at them. "Right," he says to them. "Please get these people out of the tree so we can do our job."

The police officer looks at the man with the high-vis jacket. "Well, we've come to do our job. We have to order you to remove those nets. You've disturbed a wild bird building its nest, and that's against the law!"

Once we know the Crow Tree is safe, Mum and I come down and sit with Gracie, Mia and her parents, and watch the nets being pulled off. I can't help thinking that if Mum and I hadn't sat in the tree, we wouldn't have saved Kevin. This tree would have been cut down and chopped up.

The man in the high-vis jacket is looking angry about having to work late to take the nets down, but I don't care.

Kevin doesn't care either.

He's flying in circles high above. "Caw, caw, caw!" he calls.

Then, as the evening falls, he settles with his mate, in their nest. He fluffs up his feathers and caws loudly, and I like to think he knows he's safe in his tree. The Crow Tree.

I walk to school the next day and Kevin joins me, stopping on lamp posts and rooftops.

I don't see Carter and his mates at first. They surround me and push me behind the bike shed.

Carter scowls. "Hey, Birdbrain. Think you're famous now? Just cos you've been on TV?"

Carter pushes me against the wall. He doesn't want money. He wants revenge.

"Leave me alone," I say.

"Caw ... Caw!"

Aiden picks up a stone and aims it at Kevin. "We'll finish what we started."

But then I hear Mia's voice. "Leave him alone."

Carter spins around and sees Mia.

“Just you and Ash against us?” laughs Carter.

“No,” says Mia. “There are others who don’t want to be silent any more.”

Then I see Yusef, Chloe, Ben, Omar and Luna from school step forward.

“Yeah,” agrees Yusef. “We’ve all had enough.”

“You’re going to regret this,” says Carter.

“We’ve had enough,” repeats Mia. “We’ve all reported you. You’re not going to bully anyone else again.”

I pull myself away from Carter and walk over to join Mia and the others.

Carter kicks the ground. “You’re all losers, you know that?”

Kevin is circling, cawing loudly.

Carter looks up.

And at that moment, Kevin drops a big, white bird poo. I’m sure it isn’t just luck because Kevin’s aim is far too good. It smacks Carter right in the eye.

We've saved the Crow Field for now. Loads of people signed the petition and the council has had to put any building work on hold. We'll still have to fight for it again when the birds have stopped nesting.

Now summer's almost over, and tomorrow I'll be starting at a new school with new friends. I'm glad Mia will be there too. Since we all stood up to Carter, our class has got on really well.

Mia and I are on our way to meet our school friends when we see Gracie sitting on the bench near the Crow Tree.

Gracie smiles at us. "I'm glad we can see the Crow Tree in its autumn colours again. I would miss it if it was gone."

Mia and I are about to join our friends when a tall woman walks towards us. She looks almost as old as my nan, and when she speaks, she has a German accent.

"Please can you help me?" she says. "I'm looking for Gracie."

Gracie smiles. "My name is Gracie. Do I know you?"

"No," says the woman, "but I think you knew my father. His name was Otto. Otto Meyer." She rests her arm on Gracie's arm. "He died ten years ago."

Gracie's eyes well up with tears. "I'm so sorry."

The woman smiles. "I'm sorry too. A friend here in England sent me the news about the children saving the Crow Field. I heard you being interviewed too, and heard you talk about my father.

"He always told me about the girl named Gracie and the tree that saved them that day."

"I've often thought of Otto," says Gracie. "Was he happy?"

"Yes, he was," says the woman. "After the war, he moved back to Germany to live with friends, then he settled down and got married and had me. My name is Ottoline, after him."

Kevin flies down again and paces up and down in front of us, pecking on the ground as if he wants attention.

"This is Kevin," I say. "Gracie says Otto liked crows too."

"He loved crows," said Ottoline. "He would be glad to see that you've saved Kevin. After all he suffered, he could never bear to see injustice in the world. He always said you have to fight for justice."

Kevin caws loudly again, but I see it's because he's seen Carter walking on the path.

He hates Carter as much as I do. Carter sees us and walks the other way. He's on his own, his shoulders slumped. I never see him with Josh or Aiden any more. And I think that it must be lonely being the bully. No one ever really likes you. They only stay friends because they want protection. But Carter hasn't got anyone now.

"I hate him," I mutter.

"Me too," says Mia.

Ottoline watches Carter walk away, then turns to us. "My father said you must always let go of hatred. It destroys you from the inside out. We must lead the way. We must be the change we wish to see."

I watch Carter make his way along the bottom of the field. I can see he's trying to avoid being seen by our friends on the pitch. "I still hate him," I say.

Mia stands up and pulls me up too. "Come on," she says. "What Otto said is true. It's up to us to put this right."

Mia and I walk after Carter.

"Hey, Carter," Mia shouts.

Carter turns to look at us.

Mia takes a step towards him. "Why don't you come and play football? We need another person on the team to make it even."

Carter just stares at us, like he's not sure if we're being serious.

"Yeah," I say. "Come on."

"The others won't want me," he says.

"Stay there," I say, "We'll ask them."

Mia and I walk down to the others and ask if Carter can play.

At first, they don't want him, but Mia persuades them.

I wave for Carter to join us.

He walks towards us, with the beginning of a nervous smile on his face.

And we play together, on the last day of summer, in the Crow Field.

We play until the sun sinks lower and the shadows are long across the field.

Everyone else is heading for home, but there's one last thing I've got to do. I grab my bag and walk along the path.

Kevin flies down to meet me.

"Caw, caw, caw."

The leaves on the Crow Tree are beginning to turn from green to autumn yellow.

I look up into the branches spreading out above me. Maybe this tree will live another 250 years. I wonder what this place will look like then?

But not even trees live forever.

"Caw," caws Kevin.

I smile because it's as if he knows what I'm thinking.

I reach down and pick up an acorn.

It's a seed of this oak tree.

It's a future tree.

Maybe it will live for a thousand years.

I walk up the field to an open space, where I kneel down on the grass. Kevin follows and hops on the ground beside me, watching me, like he knows what I'm about to do.

I dig my fingers into the soil.

"Caw ... Caw!" says Kevin.

I push the acorn deep into the ground.

I plant it for all the people and the crows that will come after us.

I plant the acorn, for Kevin and for me.

Chat about the book

1 Read page 42. How did the oak tree save Gracie?

2 Go to page 27. Ash uses the word 'feeble' to describe how he spoke to the man. What does 'feeble' mean?

3 Read page 13. How do you know that Ash has climbed the tree many times before?

4 Read page 30. What is meant by the sentence, 'It's like they are blindfolded.'?

5 Go to page 34. Were you surprised that Carter and his friends went away when the old lady arrived? Explain your answer with evidence from the text.

6 Look at page 52. Ash says, '"Shut up," I yell. "SHUT UP!"'. What do the words in capital letters tell you about how Ash is speaking and how he is feeling?

7 Read pages 68 and 69. How do Ash and Mia's feelings towards Carter change?

8 Imagine if you were being bullied by Carter and his friends. What would you do? What advice would you have given Ash and Mia?